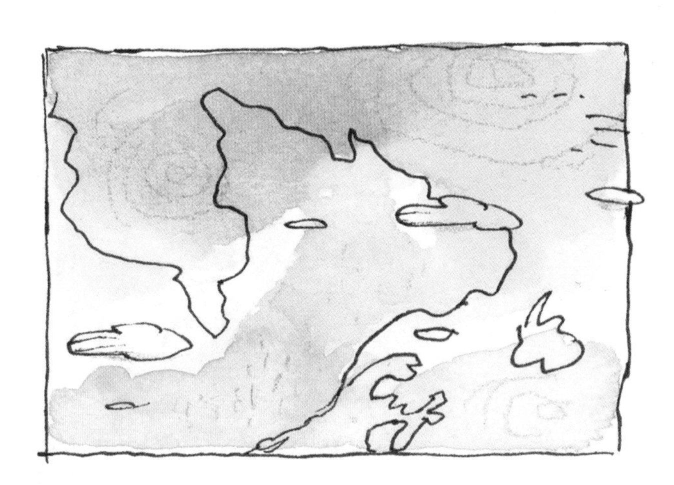

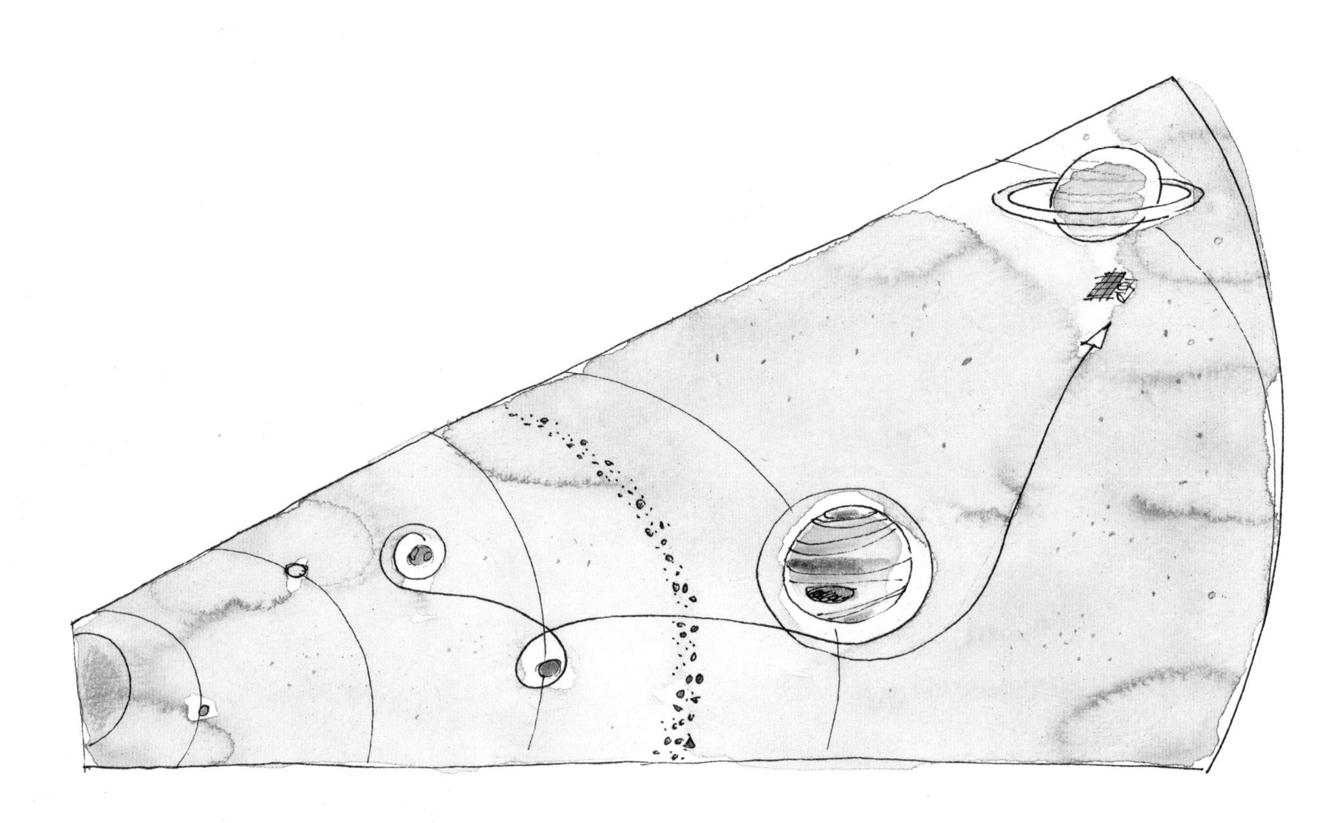

The Stars

To Galileo Galilei and to Janusz Korczak

First published in English by Greystone Books in 2023
English edition published in agreement with Koja Agency
Originally published in French in 2019 as *Les étoiles*

23 24 25 26 27 5 4 3 2 1

Aldana Libros / Greystone Books Ltd.
greystonebooks.com

Cataloguing data available from Library and Archives Canada
ISBN 978-1-77164-919-3 (cloth)
ISBN 978-1-77164-920-9 (epub)

Editing of original edition by Liette Lemay
Jacket and interior design by Martin Brault, Stéphane Ulrich, and Jessica Sullivan

Printed and bound in China on FSC® certified paper at Shenzhen Reliance Printing. The FSC® label means that materials used for the product have been responsibly sourced.

Greystone Books thanks the Canada Council for the Arts, the British Columbia Arts Council, the Province of British Columbia through the Book Publishing Tax Credit, and the Government of Canada for supporting our publishing activities.

Canada

Greystone Books gratefully acknowledges the xʷməθkʷəy̓əm (Musqueam), Sḵwx̱wú7mesh (Squamish), and səl̓ilwətaɬ (Tsleil-Waututh) peoples on whose land our Vancouver head office is located.

Jacques Goldstyn

TRANSLATED BY HELEN MIXTER

The Stars

ALDANA LIBROS

VANCOUVER / BERKELEY / LONDON

My name is Yakov.
I have three sisters: Sarah, Rivka, and Fanny.
Me, I'm the oldest.

Every day I take my sisters to the park.
They want me to play with them, but I think their games are silly, and anyway they always end up quarreling. They drive me crazy.

I prefer to read. I love space.
I know that one day I'll go to the Moon,
to Mars, to Titan, or to Ganymede.

In the meantime, I make rocket ships out of tin cans and yogurt cups.
USA
Yakov! You're wasting your time. You'd do better to spend your time on important things.
USA

My father has a grocery store, and he has decided that I'll take over the business when I grow up.

I think Dad is right. They say that Mum's grandfather was a daydreamer, a crazy kind of poet who played a fiddle on the roof.

My mother is the opposite of my father. She is sweet and gentle. When we are with her, we laugh and sing all the time.

I don't think she gives a hoot whether I become a grocer or not.

She just wants me to be happy.

Yankele, stop getting on your father's nerves. That's all I ask. Try not to be on the Moon when you are supposed to be looking after your sisters.
STAR WARS
STAR WARS
Sometimes being on the Moon is very nice, but it can get lonely.
STAR WARS

Then one day, at the park...

You should know that no one in my family walks around in bare feet. Boys wear boots and girls wear flat slippers. But never, ever sandals!

These are the most beautiful feet I have ever seen in all my life. The toes are regular and go down in perfect order by size. And the nails are like tiny computer screens.

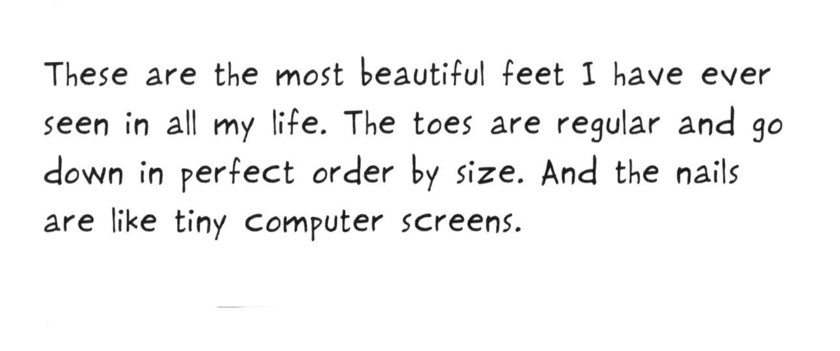

In comparison, I have totally uneven toes that look like the battlements on a castle.

The owner of those beautiful feet is a girl my age who also has a pretty face.
It is the first time I've seen this girl. A bunch of her brothers are jumping all around her.
WOW!

I rub my eyes...
I look closely...
She's reading a book about space!!
SPACE
Then she looks up. Her eyes are black-black like two little asteroids.

She notices me, my book, and my astonished face. Her face lights up with a beautiful smile. Her teeth are just as regular as her toenails.

And that is how I met Aïcha.

Gefiltefish & fils
CCCP

And the most incredible thing is that her family has just moved into the house right behind ours!

There's no point in saying that no one has to beg me to take my sisters to the park ever again!

We spend hours talking about space.
I am mainly interested in spaceships.

And Aïcha knows so much about the stars, the galaxies, the universe.
Soon we are inseparable, like twin stars. I feel like I'm in orbit around her.

Together we go to the neighborhood library.

We empty out the astronomy shelves.

After the library, I take Aïcha to get her first bagel.

I have a sesame bagel. She has a poppy seed one.

Then Aïcha takes me to eat ice cream at Bill Bockett's. I'd never set a foot in there before. I order pecan chocolate chip. She orders maple syrup.

People gossip about our friendship.

But we aren't to be gossiped about.

We have become best friends.

When I am with her, everything seems easier.

I don't notice time going by anymore.

Salade

You see that star? It's Deneb.
And those are Altair and Vega.
Those stars were named by Arab astronomers in the Middle Ages.
And that's the Great Bear.
Yes, I know that one. It looks like a dipper.
Look at the second star on the handle.
?

Alcor
Mizar
It's not one star but TWO stars side by side.
You're right! I can see them!!
That proves you've got good eyesight. They say that to be an archer in Genghis Khan's army, you had to be able to tell them apart with your bare eyes.
Aïcha takes my hand and points my finger at other stars. But leaning against her in the bowl of the hammock, with my cheek so close to hers, I can't see anything anymore.

Gently, her veil slips off her shoulders and a waterfall of curls bursts out like an intergalactic cloud.

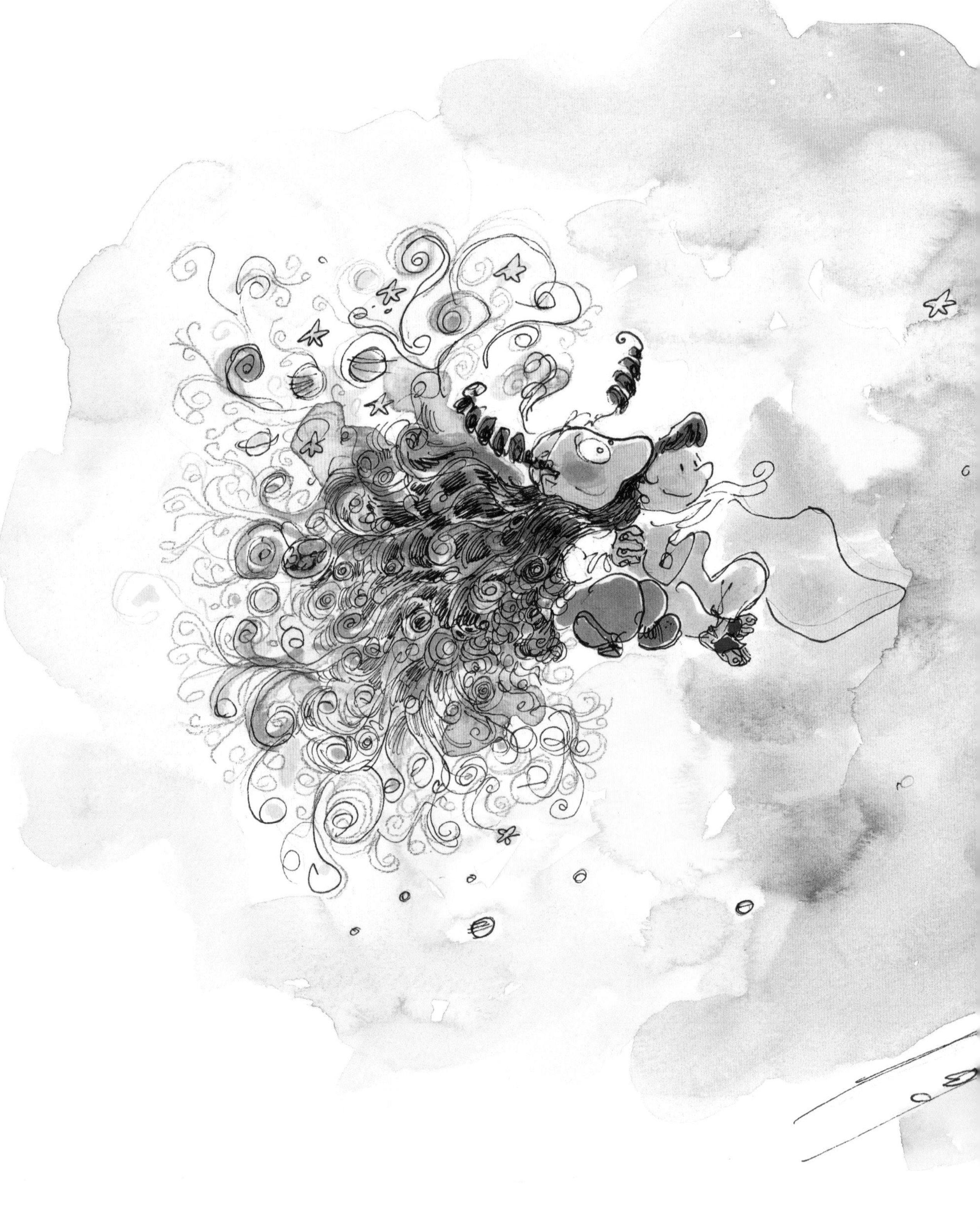

At that moment, a huge yell makes us leap into the air.
It is Aïcha's father.

I flee at the speed of light, as if I have been struck by lightning.

The next day, it is impossible to see Aïcha.
No one answers when I knock on the door.

She doesn't come to the park anymore.

Things are very bad. My dad and Aïcha's fight about us.

But a few days later, they agree on one thing. To build a wall.

Days and weeks pass without my seeing Aïcha.
I am o-blit-er-ated.

Secretly, I begin to dig a tunnel.

Aïcha has moved out.

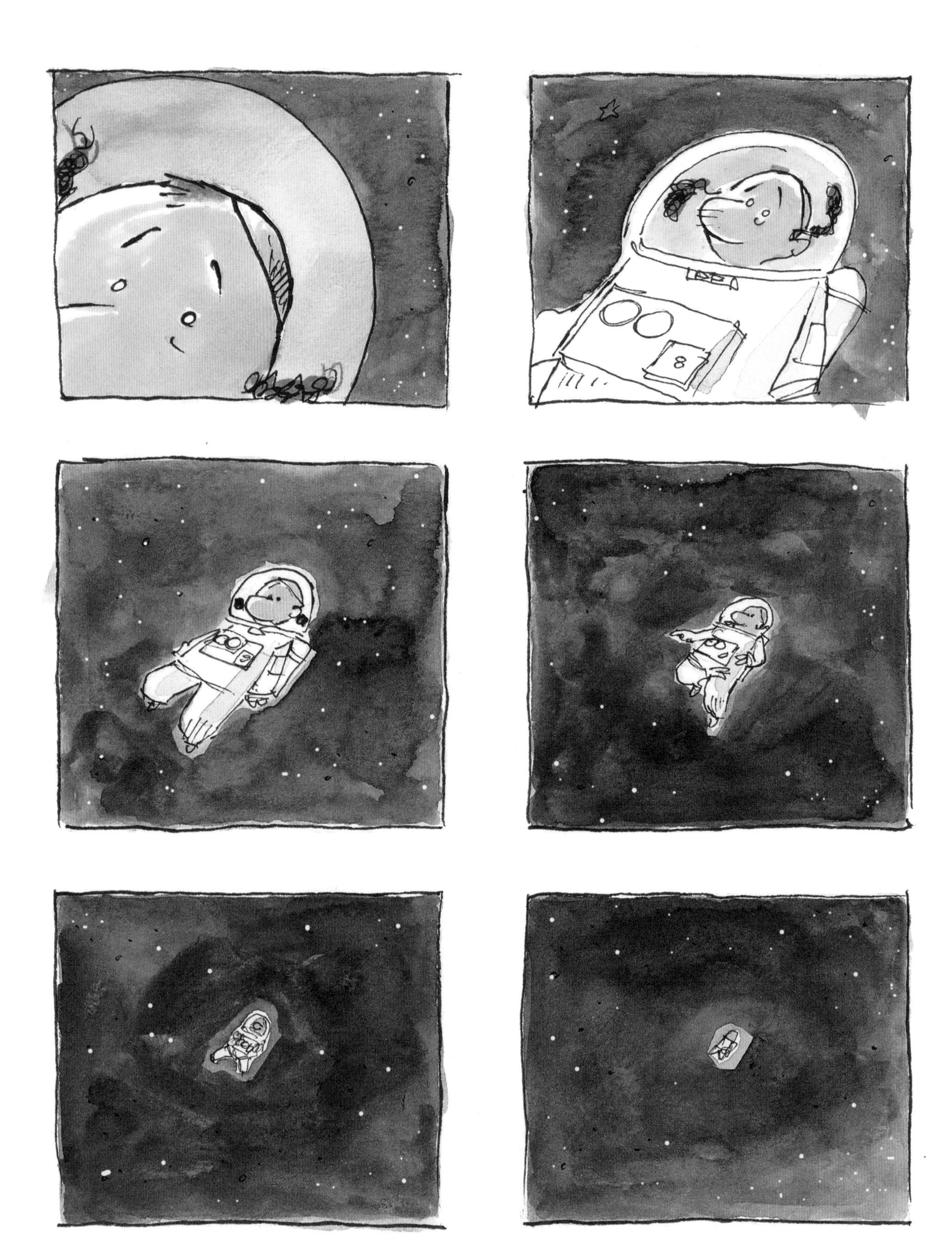

AÏCHA

Years go by. Many years. Against my father's wishes, I study science, especially physics and chemistry.

Université de Montréal
Physiqu
NX87

I achieve my dream. I work at NASA
and I build space probes.

I calculate their paths toward planets like Saturn and Jupiter, and even farther.

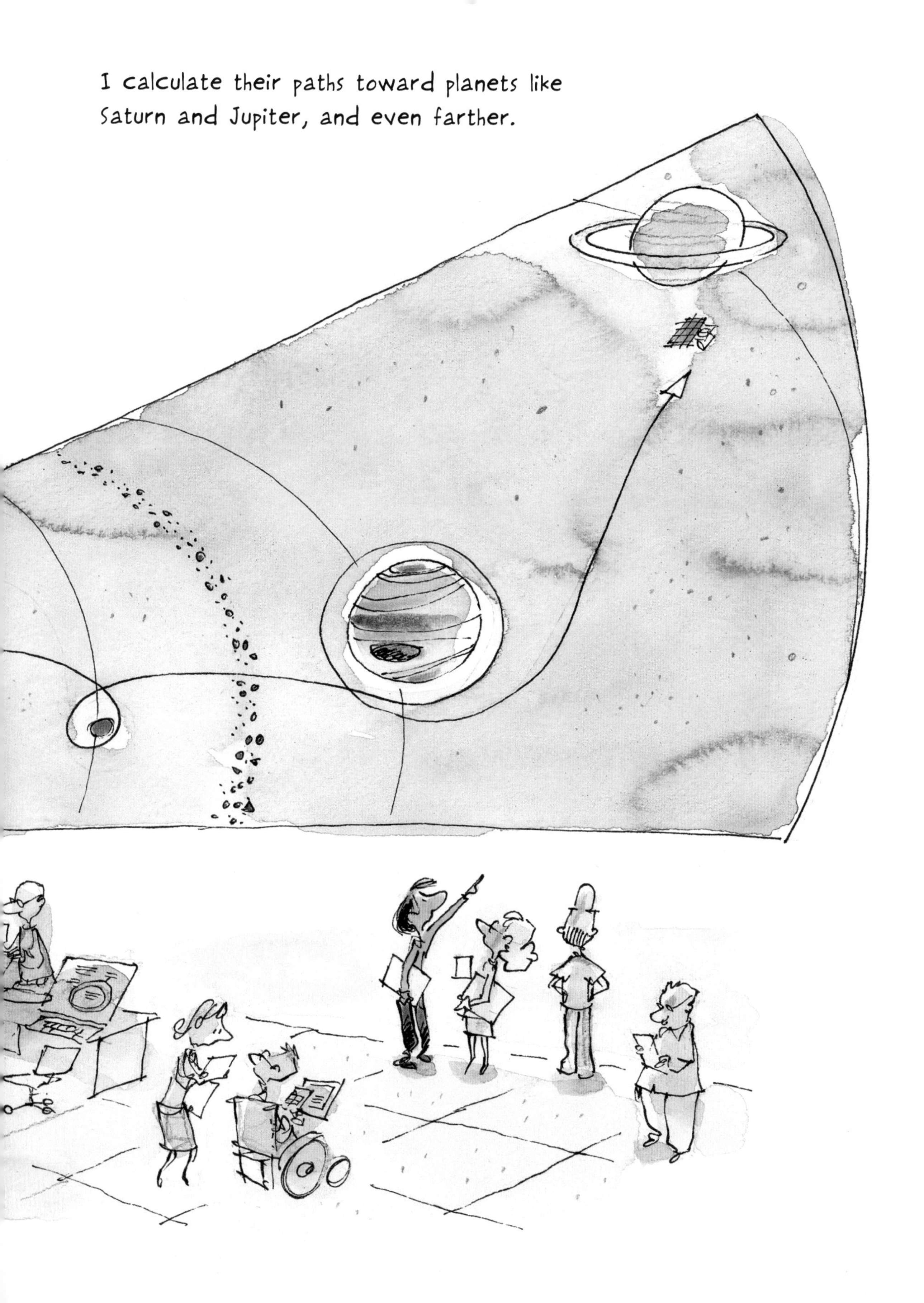

And then, one day, when I am at a huge international astronomy conference...

KONFERENZ ÜBER ASTRONOMIE
BERLIN

Aïcha!
We jump into each other's arms.
We hug each other.

She still smells as sweet as ever, like jasmine.

We have so much to tell each other and lost time to make up. We talk and talk...

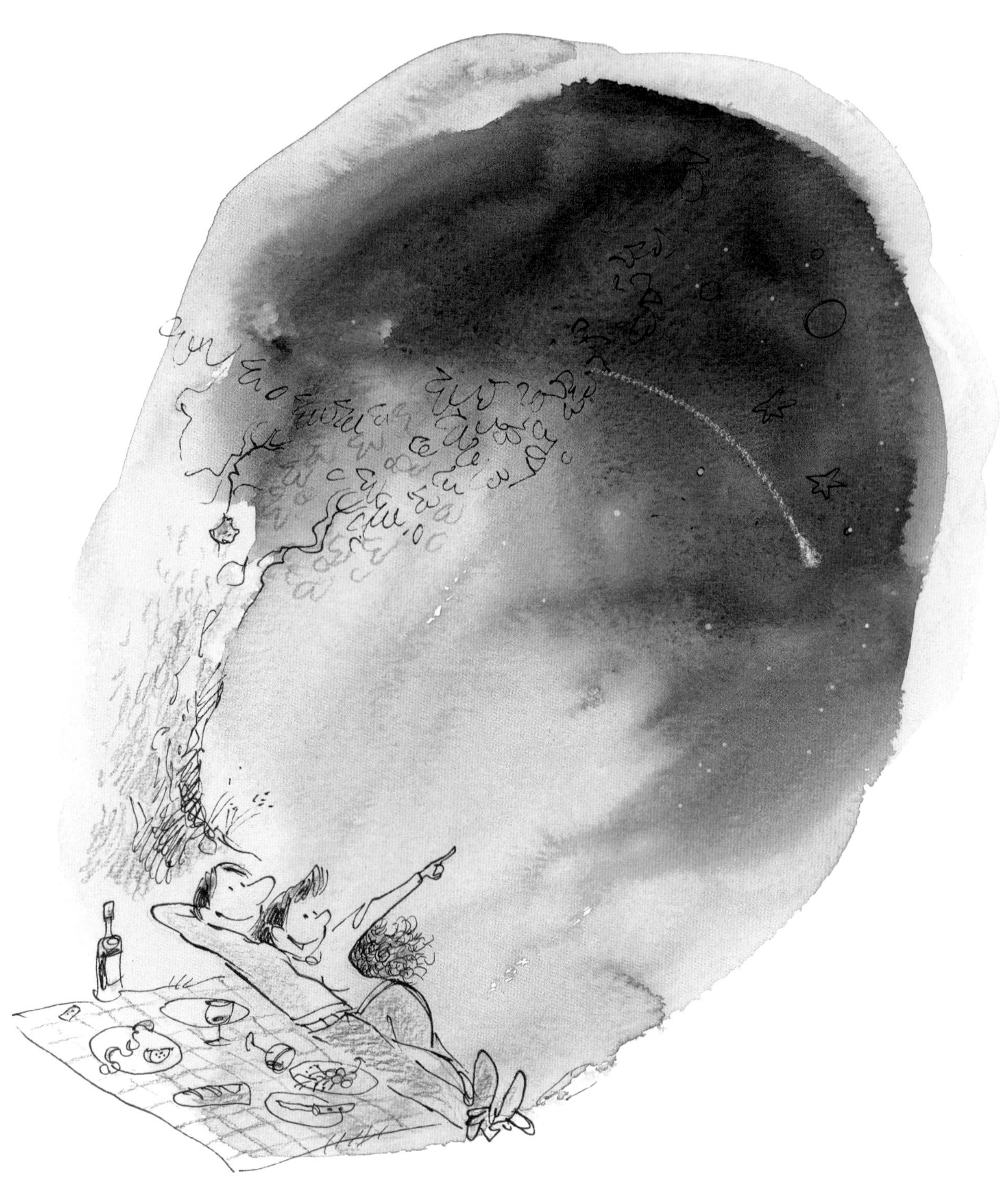

...and since that day we have never been apart.

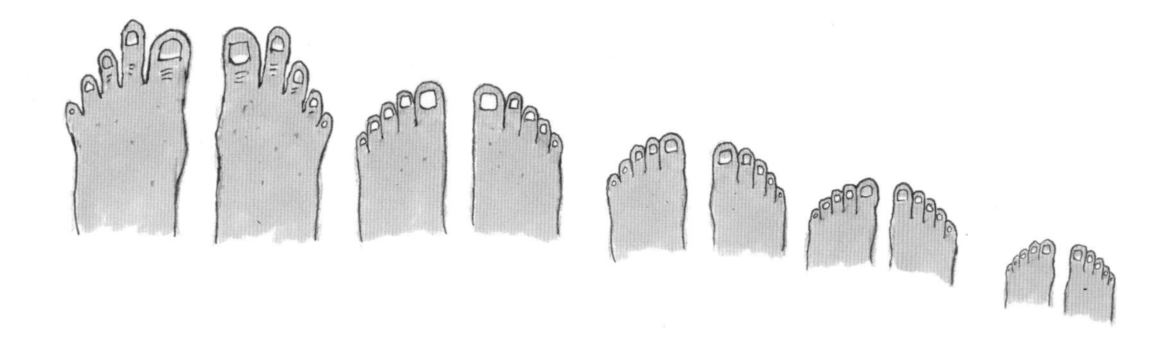